# Gooney Bird Greene

# Gooney Bird Greene

## LOIS LOWRY

## Illustrated by Middy Thomas

Houghton Mifflin Company Boston 2002

Walter Lorraine Books

For Beanie and Chelsea, from their grandmas
— L.L. and M.T.

Walter Lorraine (wr) Books

Text Copyright © 2002 by Lois Lowry
Illustrations by Middy Thomas Copyright © 2002 by Houghton
Mifflin Company

www.houghtonmifflinbooks.com

*Library of Congress Cataloging-in-Publication Data*

Lowry, Lois.
  Gooney Bird Greene / Lois Lowry : illustrated by Middy Thomas.
    p. cm.
Summary: A most unusual new student who loves to be the center of
attention entertains her teacher and fellow second-graders by telling
absolutely true stories about herself, including how she got her name.
  ISBN 0-618-23848-4
  [1. Storytelling—Fiction. 2. Schools—Fiction. 3. Humorous stories.]
I. Thomas, Middy Chilman, 1931– ill. II. Title.
  PZ7.L9673 Go 2002
  [Fic]—dc21

                                                      2002001478

Printed in the United States of America
VB  10  9  8  7  6  5  4  3  2  1

# Gooney Bird Greene

**1.**

There was a new student in the Watertower Elementary School. She arrived in October, after the first month of school had already passed. She opened the second grade classroom door at ten o'clock on a Wednesday morning and appeared there all alone, without even a mother to introduce her. She was wearing pajamas and cowboy boots and was holding a dictionary and a lunch box.

"Hello," Mrs. Pidgeon, the second grade teacher, said. "We're in the middle of our spelling lesson."

"Good," said the girl in pajamas. "I brought my dictionary. Where's my desk?"

"Who are you?" Mrs. Pidgeon asked politely.

"I'm your new student. My name is Gooney Bird Greene — that's Greene with a silent 'e' at the end — and I just moved here from China. I want a desk right smack in the middle of the room, because I like to be right smack in the middle of everything."

The class stared at the new girl with admiration. They had never met anyone like Gooney Bird Greene.

She was a good student. She sat down at the desk Mrs. Pidgeon provided, right smack in the middle of everything, and began doing second grade spelling. She did all her work neatly and quickly, and she followed instructions.

But soon it was clear that Gooney Bird was mysterious and interesting. Her clothes were unusual. Her hairstyles were unusual. Even her lunches were very unusual.

At lunchtime on Wednesday, her first day in the school, she opened her lunch box and brought out sushi and a pair of bright green chopsticks. On Thursday, her second day at Watertower Elementary School, Gooney Bird Greene was wearing a pink ballet tutu over green stretch pants, and she had three small red grapes, an avocado, and an oatmeal cookie for lunch.

On Thursday afternoon, after lunch, Mrs. Pidgeon stood in front of the class with a piece of chalk in her hand. "Today," she said, "we are going to continue talking about stories."

"Yay!" the second-graders said in very loud voices, all but Felicia Ann, who never spoke, and Malcolm, who wasn't paying attention. He was under his desk, as usual.

"Gooney Bird, you weren't here for the first month of school. But our class has been learning about what makes good stories, haven't we?" Mrs. Pidgeon said. Everyone

nodded. All but Malcolm, who was under his desk doing something with scissors.

"Class? What does a story need most of all? Who remembers?" Mrs. Pidgeon had her chalk hand in the air, ready to write something on the board.

The children were silent for a minute. They were thinking. Finally Chelsea raised her hand.

"Chelsea? What does a story need?"

"A book," Chelsea said.

Mrs. Pidgeon put her chalk hand down. "There are many stories that don't need a book," she said pleasantly, "aren't there, class? If your grandma tells you a story about when she was a little girl, she doesn't have that story in a book, does she?"

The class stared at her. All but Malcolm, who was still under his desk, and Felicia Ann, who always looked at the floor, never raised her hand, and never spoke.

Beanie said, "My grandma lives in Boston!"

Keiko said, "My grandma lives in Honolulu!"

Ben said loudly, "My grandma lives in Harrisburg, Pennsylvania!"

Tricia shouted, "My grandma is very rich!"

"*Class!*" said Mrs. Pidgeon. "Shhh!" Then, in a quieter voice, she explained, "Another time, we will talk about our families. But right now —" She stopped talking and looked at Barry Tuckerman. Barry was up on his knees in his seat,

and his hand was waving in the air as hard as he could make it wave.

"Barry?" Mrs. Pidgeon said. "Do you have something that you simply have to say? Something that cannot possibly wait?"

Barry nodded yes. His hand waved.

"And what is so important?"

Barry stood up beside his desk. Barry Tuckerman liked to make very important speeches, and they always required that he stand.

"My grandma," Barry Tuckerman said, "went to jail once. She was twenty years old and she went to jail for civil dis-obedience." Then Barry sat down.

"Thank you, Barry. Now look at what I'm writing on the board. Who can read this word?"

Everyone, all but Malcolm and Felicia Ann, watched as she wrote the long word. Then they shouted it out. "BEGIN-NING!"

"Good!" said Mrs. Pidgeon. "Now I'm sure you'll all know this one." She wrote again.

"MIDDLE!" the children shouted.

"Good. And can you guess what the last word will be?" She held up her chalk and waited.

"END!"

"Correct!" Mrs. Pidgeon said. "Good for you, second-graders! Those are the parts that a story needs: a beginning, a middle, and an end. Now I'm gong to write another very long word on the board. Let's see what good readers you are." She wrote a C, then an H.

"Mrs. Pidgeon!" someone called.

She wrote an A, and then an R.

*"MRS. PIDGEON!"* Several children were calling now.

She turned to see what was so important. Malcolm was standing beside his desk. He was crying.

"Malcolm needs to go to the nurse, Mrs. Pidgeon!" Beanie said.

Mrs. Pidgeon went to Malcolm and knelt beside him. "What's the trouble, Malcolm?" she asked. But he couldn't stop crying.

"I know, I know!" Nicholas said. Nicholas always knew everything, and his desk was beside Malcolm's.

"Tell me, Nicholas."

"Remember Keiko showed us how to make origami stars?"

All of the second-graders reached into their desks and their pockets and their lunch boxes. There were tiny stars everywhere. Keiko had shown them how to make origami stars out of small strips of paper. The stars were very easy to make. The school janitor had complained just last Friday that he was sweeping up hundreds of origami stars.

"Malcolm put one in his nose," Nicholas said, "and now he can't get it out."

"Is that correct, Malcolm?" Mrs. Pidgeon asked. Malcolm nodded and wiped his eyes.

"Don't sniff, Malcolm. *Do not sniff.* That is an order." She took his hand and walked with him to the classroom door. She turned to the class. "Children," she said, "I am going to be gone for exactly one minute and thirty seconds while I walk with Malcolm to the nurse's office down the hall. Stay in your seats while I'm gone. Think about the word *character.*

"A character is what a story needs. When I come back from the nurse's office, we are going to create a story together. You must choose who the main character will be. Talk among yourselves quietly. Think about interesting characters like Abraham Lincoln, or perhaps Christopher Columbus, or —"

"Babe Ruth?" called Ben.

"Yes, Babe Ruth is a possibility. I'll be right back."

Mrs. Pidgeon left the classroom with Malcolm.

When she returned, one minute and thirty seconds later, without Malcolm, the class was waiting. They had been whispering, all but Felicia Ann, who never whispered.

"Have you chosen?" she asked. The class nodded. All of their heads went up and down, except Felicia Ann's, because she always looked at the floor.

"And your choice is —?"

All of the children, all but Felicia Ann, called out together. "Gooney Bird Greene!" they called.

Mrs. Pidgeon sighed. "Class," she said, "there are many different kinds of stories. There are stories about imaginary creatures, like —"

"Dumbo!" Tricia called out.

"Raise your hand if you want to speak, please," Mrs. Pidgeon said. "But yes, Tricia, you are correct. Dumbo is an imaginary character. There are also stories about real people from history, like Christopher Columbus, and —" She stopped. Barry Tuckerman was waving and waving his hand. "Yes, Barry? Do you have something very important to say?"

Barry Tuckerman stood up. He twisted the bottom of his shirt around and around in his fingers. "I forget," he said at last.

"Well, sit back down then, Barry. Now, I thought, class, that since Christopher Columbus's birthday is coming up soon —" She looked at Barry Tuckerman, whose hand was waving like a windmill once again. "Barry?" she said.

Barry Tuckerman stood up again. "We already know all the stories about Christopher Columbus," he said. "We want to hear a true story about Gooney Bird Greene."

"Yes! Gooney Bird Greene!" the class called.

Mrs. Pidgeon sighed again. "I'm afraid I don't know many facts abut Gooney Bird Greene," she said. "I know a *lot* of facts about Christopher Columbus, though. Christopher Columbus was born in —"

*"We want Gooney Bird!"* the class chanted.

"Gooney Bird?" Mrs. Pidgeon said, finally. "How do you feel about this?"

Gooney Bird Greene stood up beside her desk in the middle of the room. "Can I tell the story?" she asked. "Can I be right smack in the middle of everything? Can I be the hero?"

"Well, since you would be the main character," Mrs. Pidgeon said, "I guess that would put you in the middle of everything. I guess that would make you the hero."

"Good," Gooney Bird said. "I will tell you an absolutely true story about me."

## 2.

Gooney Bird adjusted the pink ballet tutu she was wearing over a pair of green stretch pants. Her T-shirt was decorated with polka dots. Her red hair was pulled into two pigtails and held there with blue scrunchies.

She pulled carefully on one of her pigtails, rearranging it neatly, because the scrunchie was coming loose. She felt her earlobes, which were small and pink and empty.

"I should have worn the dangling diamond earrings that I got from the prince," she told the class. "Maybe I'll wear them next week."

*"Diamond earrings? Prince?"* Mrs. Pidgeon asked.

"Well, actually, the prince didn't give me the earrings. I got them at the palace," Gooney Bird explained.

"Why were you at the palace?"

"Well, first I was in jail, and then —" Gooney Bird interrupted herself. "It's a long story." She reached down and tidied her socks.

11

"May I come up to the front of the room to begin?" she asked the teacher after she had adjusted her clothes. "I like to be absolutely the center of attention."

Mrs. Pidgeon nodded and stepped aside so that there was room for Gooney Bird to stand in the front of the class.

"You might as well sit down, Mrs. Pidgeon," Gooney Bird said politely. "Take a load off your feet."

Mrs. Pidgeon sat down in the chair behind her cluttered desk. She looked at the clock on the wall. "We have fifteen minutes," she said, "before arithmetic."

"Class," Gooney Bird said, "you heard Mrs. Pidgeon. We have just fifteen minutes. There are many Gooney Bird stories I might tell you, but I have time for only one today. Who has a suggestion for a story?"

Ben's hand shot up. "Tell about how you came from China," he said.

Nicholas called, "Why are you named Gooney Bird?"

Chelsea was wiggling and wiggling in her seat. "The palace!" she said. "Tell about jail, and the palace, and the diamond earrings!"

Other hands were waving, but Gooney Bird motioned for those children to put their hands down. She looked around the room, thinking.

"This is the title of the story," she said at last. "'How Gooney Bird Got Her Name.'"

"Just like *How the Leopard Got His Spots,*" Barry

Tuckerman said in a loud whisper.

"Barry, pay attention, please," Gooney Bird said. "I like to have absolutely all eyes on me." Then, when the class was silent, and all eyes, except those of Felicia Ann, who always looked at the floor, were on her, she began.

## How Gooney Bird Got Her Name

Once upon a time, eight years ago, a man and a woman named Mr. and Mrs. Greene — that's Greene with a silent 'e' at the end — discovered that they were expecting a baby girl.

The man's name was Gordon Greene. His wife was Barbara Greene.

They decided to name their baby girl with their initials. G for Gordon, B for Barbara.

They thought of many different names.

"Gail Beth," said Mrs. Greene. She liked short names.

"Gwendolyn Belinda," said Mr. Greene. He liked long names.

They discussed and discussed. They never

argued or fought. But they had many discussions.

Once, in the middle of the night, Mrs. Greene woke up. She had had a dream about a name. She nudged Mr. Greene until he woke up a little bit. Then she said, "Georgina Babette."

"No," he said, and went back to sleep.

One night Mr. Greene woke up, nudged his wife, and told her that he had had a dream. "Gazpacho Banana," he said.

"That was a nightmare you had," his wife said. He agreed. They both went back to sleep.

Finally, because they could not make up their minds about a name, they decided that they would wait until the baby girl was born. Then they would look at the baby and somehow they would know that her name should be Grace Bridget, or Gloria Bonnie, or some other name.

They waited and waited for the baby's birth. It takes many months, as you know.

Gooney Bird paused in her story. She could see that many of the children wanted to wave their hands in the air and say things.

15

"Class?" she said. "Any comments so far? Any questions?"

"We have nine minutes left," Mrs. Pidgeon reminded them, "before arithmetic."

Keiko asked in a small voice, "Did he really say Gazpacho Banana?"

"Yes, he did," Gooney Bird said. "I tell only absolutely true stories."

Barry Tuckerman stood up beside his desk. "I was named a B name for my grandfather," he said. "My grandfather's name was Benjamin."

"That's *my* name!" Ben called out.

"My grandfather was in college when my grandmother went to jail," Barry added, "or he would have gone with her."

Tricia raised her hand. "My cat's name is Fluffernutter," she said.

"Four more minutes!" Mrs. Pidgeon announced. "Let's let Gooney Bird get back to her story so that we can hear the ending.

"Did you notice, class," she added, "how she uses *characters* and *dialogue*? And her story is full of suspense. It's a cliffhanger, isn't it? What a good storyteller Gooney Bird is!"

"Ready?" Gooney Bird asked.

"Ready!" shouted the class, all but Felicia Ann, who never shouted.

"Okay. Here comes the ending."

Finally, one spring morning, the baby girl was born. She weighed six pounds and fourteen ounces. She had red hair.

"Look!" said her mother. "She wiggles her head around, looking for food when she's hungry. Isn't that cute! It reminds me of something, but I forget what."

Her father peered down at the new baby in his wife's arms. He smiled. "She has very big feet! Isn't that cute! It reminds me of something, but I forget what."

Mr. and Mrs. Greene looked at their sweet baby. They thought and thought.

"It's coming back to me," Mr. Greene said at last. "Do you remember when we went on that bird-watching trip to various islands in the Pacific Ocean, and we saw all kinds of marine birds?"

"That's it!" his wife said. "She looks very much like one of those birds. But which one?"

"Let's get our photograph album from that trip," Mr. Greene said.

Together they turned the pages of the album.

"Doubled-crested cormorant?" Mrs. Greene said. They looked down at the baby. No. She didn't look like a double-crested cormorant.

"Red-necked grebe?" Mr. Greene suggested. They looked at the baby again.

"She *does* have a red neck," Mr. Greene said.

"She does not!" said Mrs. Greene. "It's pink."

They turned the pages some more. Suddenly they both said, "Oh!"

Very carefully they looked at the photograph. Then very carefully they looked at the baby.

"Big feet," Mr. Green said. "Just like our baby's."

"A head that bobs around," Mrs. Greene said. "Just like our baby's."

"That's the one," they agreed.

They read the label under the photograph. "Laysan Albatross," the label said.

"I don't think Laysan Albatross Greene is a very pretty name for a baby girl," Mrs. Greene said sadly. "It sounds too scientific."

"I agree," Mr. Greene said. "But look at the small print."

Together Mr. and Mrs. Greene read the words in the small print: *OFFEN CALLED GOONEY BIRD.*

"Gooney Bird Greene!" they said.

"I like the sound of it!" Mrs. Greene said. "And it has a G and a B."

"It does indeed," said Mr. Greene.

So they decided to name their new baby girl Gooney Bird Greene. Then everyone, including a doctor, a midwife, and a cleaning lady, hugged and kissed and did a Viennese waltz together.

The End

"What a lovely story!" Mrs. Pidgeon said. "And it gives us a chance do some science research. We will look up 'Laysan Albatross' in the encyclopedia. Thank you, Gooney Bird. You may take your seat now, and we'll turn to our arithmetic."

"Wait! Wait!" Beanie's hand was waving in the air.

"Yes, Beanie?" Mrs. Pidgeon asked. "What's wrong?"

"I want to hear about the diamond earrings, and the palace!"

"That's a different story," Gooney Bird said. She was walking back to her desk.

"Tell it! Tell it!" the children called.

Barry Tuckerman jumped up and stood beside his desk. "I want to hear how Gooney Bird came from China!" he said.

"I came on a flying carpet," Gooney Bird said. "But that's a different story, too." She adjusted her pink tutu and sat down.

"Tell it! Tell it!" the children called.

Mrs. Pidgeon laughed. "I'm sure Gooney Bird was just joking about the prince and the palace and the diamond earrings," she said, "and the flying carpet, too."

Gooney Bird had already opened her arithmetic book. She looked up in surprise. "No," she said. "I wasn't joking. I tell only absolutely true stories."

"Well," said Mrs. Pidgeon, "will you tell us another tomorrow?"

"Of course," Gooney Bird said.

**3.**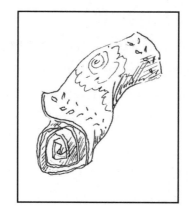

On Friday, Gooney Bird was wearing Capri pants, a satin tank top, and a long string of pearls. Her red hair was twisted into one long braid, which was decorated with plastic flowers. There were flip-flops on her feet.

"You look beautiful," Keiko said to Gooney Bird in an admiring whisper.

"Yes, I know," Gooney Bird replied. "Thank you, Keiko." She walked to the front of the classroom when Mrs. Pidgeon told her it was time.

Malcolm was back in the classroom. He was at his desk, writing "I will never put anything in my nose" one hundred times on a piece of lined paper. The nurse had told him to do that. She said it would keep his hands busy.

"How come Gooney Bird gets to go stand in front of the class?" Malcolm asked.

"Shhhhh," everybody, except Felicia Ann, said to Malcolm. *"Listen."*

"Today," Gooney Bird said, "I have a very exciting story to tell you. In my story there is a long journey, a mystery, and a rescue."

Mrs. Pidgeon, seated at her desk, had begun correcting some spelling papers. She looked up. "Listen, second-graders," she said. "Hear the different things that Gooney Bird is putting into her story? That is what good storytellers do."

Gooney Bird listened patiently to the teacher. Then she stood up straight and did some breathing exercises. Finally she took a deep breath and looked at the class. "I am ready to begin," she said at last. "The title of the story for today will be 'How Gooney Bird Came from China on a Flying Carpet.'"

"Just like Aladdin," Barry Tuckerman said in a loud whisper.

"Barry, pay attention, please," Gooney Bird said. "I like to have absolutely all eyes on me." Then, when the class became silent — all except Felicia Ann, who had been silent all along — and almost all eyes, even Mrs. Pidgeon's, were on her, she began.

## How Gooney Bird Came from China
## on a Flying Carpet

Once upon a time, just last month, Mr. and Mrs. Greene decided to take their little girl, Gooney Bird, and move away from the place where they had always lived.

They had always lived in China. But now Mr. Greene had a new job, and his new job was in Watertower.

"That's here!" Chelsea said aloud. "*I* live in Watertower!"

Gooney Bird stopped talking. She arranged her pearl necklace so that it was draped over one shoulder.

"*Me too!*" Tricia said.

"We *all* live in Watertower!" Ben pointed out. "That's why we go to the Watertower Elementary School."

"Class —" Mrs. Pidgeon warned.

"Mrs. Pidgeon," Gooney Bird said politely, "let me take care of this.

"Children," she said in a firm voice, "I cannot tell a story if I am constantly interrupted. There will be time for questions and comments. Please raise your hand if you want to say something. It's very distracting for me if you call out."

"Sorry," Tricia said.

"Sorry," Chelsea said.

"Sorry," Ben added.

The class waited. Gooney Bird looked at them all sternly. Then she did some breathing exercises and began again.

They had always lived in China. But now Mr. Greene had a new job, and his new job was in Watertower.

So they packed carefully. It took many days. First Mr. Greene had to pack forty-three sets of false teeth. Then Mrs. Greene had to pack her dancing shoes and her bathing suits. And Gooney Bird had to pack all of her belongings, which included a money collection.

Finally their furniture was loaded onto a moving van, and the Greene family waved goodbye as the moving van drove away from China and started its journey to Watertower.

Gooney Bird stopped. Every child in the classroom had a hand raised. And even Mrs. Pidgeon was waving her arm.

"I'll have an intermission now, for questions," Gooney Bird said. "Chelsea? Yours first."

"Why did Mr. Greene have forty-three pairs of false teeth?" Chelsea asked.

"The false teeth are not part of this story," Gooney Bird said. "Malcolm?"

Malcolm had looked up from his "I will not put anything in my nose" paper. His eyes were very wide. "Tell about the money collection!" he said.

"That's another story," Gooney Bird said. "Beanie?"

"When are you going to tell about the prince and the diamonds?" Beanie asked.

Gooney Bird thought it over. "On Monday I'll tell it," she said. "Now, there's time for one more question before I continue. Mrs. Pidgeon? Did you have your hand raised?"

Mrs. Pidgeon nodded. "Gooney Bird," she said in a nice voice, "you have an amazing imagination and we think you are wonderful at telling stories. Don't we, class?" She looked around, and almost all of the children nodded.

"But I want to be certain that the children understand that these are made-up stories. So I want to point out —"

"My stories are all absolutely true," Gooney Bird said.

"I want to point out," Mrs. Pidegon went on, "that of course we all know that China is a foreign country across the ocean, and that a moving van could never drive from China to Watertower."

Gooney Bird rearranged her pearls and sighed. "Mrs. Pidgeon," she said, "why don't we take a few minutes for research? Is there an atlas in the bookcase?"

Mrs. Pidgeon laughed and said, "Of course." She went to the bookcase and took out a book of maps called an atlas.

"Now," said Gooney Bird, "would you find out if there are *other* Chinas?"

"Other Chinas? I don't think —" Mrs. Pidgeon began turning the pages of the atlas. She found the index at the back.

"My goodness!" Mrs. Pidgeon said after a minute. "There's a China in Texas!"

"Correct," said Gooney Bird. "And? What else?"

"There's a China in Maine!"

"Correct," said Gooney Bird. "And?"

"California! There's a China *Lake*! Oh, and my goodness, look! In North Carolina —"

"And now it is time to continue the story," Gooney Bird announced. "Where were we? Oh, yes. I remember. The moving van had just left China —"

She took up the story again.

After the moving van left China, the Greene family loaded up their station wagon with five big suitcases. Then they added a lawn mower that they had forgotten to put in the moving van, a cooler full of ham sandwiches and iced tea, a bundled-up stack of *National Geographic*s, and an orange and white cat named Catman, who had no tail because he had flicked his former tail once under the lawn mower. The last thing they put into the station wagon was a rolled-up rug from the front porch of their house. It was too long to fit. They tried it sideways, and folded, and upside down, but it still wouldn't fit.

"Let's leave it behind," Mr. Greene suggested.

But Mrs. Greene began to cry. "It was my mother's," she said. "There's a stain on it where my mother spilled some black bean soup forty years ago. I feel sentimental about this rug."

So Mr. Greene agreed to take the rug because it made him cry, too, if his wife cried. He decided to put the back window of the station wagon down so that the end of the rolled-up rug could stick out. He made certain that everything was nicely arranged and that Catman had a comfortable place to sleep on the back seat, just beneath the end of the rug and next to the place where Gooney Bird would sit.

Mr. Greene and Mrs. Greene and Gooney Bird

Greene all got into the car and drove away from China, starting their long journey to Watertower.

They drove for many, many hours. They ate all of the ham sandwiches and drank all of the iced tea. They stopped to get gas. They went to the bathroom. They played the car radio and listened to news and operas and football games and talk shows about love relationships.

Suddenly Gooney Bird glanced down and noticed with dismay that her beloved Catman had disappeared. She looked around the floor of the back seat, but Catman was not there.

She heard a small sound, like a purr, coming from inside the rolled-up rug. She knew that Catman had entered the rug. He probably found it a warm and dark and cozy place.

But Gooney Bird was worried about Catman. She decided to try to get him out. She reached into the rolled-up center of the rug. But he slithered away, beyond her hands.

She looked at the backs of her parents' heads, wondering if she should tell them about the problem with Catman. But her mother was dozing and her father was driving, watching the road carefully and listening to a radio program about whales.

So Gooney Bird decided to wiggle into the rug herself to rescue Catman.

"Oh, no!" Keiko cried. "I'm going to faint!"
"Shhhh," the other children said.

It was dark and dusty and a very tight squeeze inside the rolled-up rug. But Gooney Bird wiggled inch by inch toward Catman.

Catman slithered away, inch by inch. She could see his glittering eyes as he backed away from her hands. Gooney Bird was determined to rescue him. She continued forward.

Suddenly an amazing thing happened. Even though Gooney Bird was not very large and did not weigh very much — and was not wearing her heavy diamond earrings from the palace that day — her weight inside the rolled-up rug caused it to tilt. At that moment, Mr. Greene leaned forward to change the radio station, and the car went over a pothole in the road. The rolled-up rug, containing both Catman and Gooney Bird, slid out of the back of the station wagon and flew through the air before it landed at the side of the road in some thick grass beside a fence post. A cow chewing a purple flower looked curiously at it and then wandered away.

The station wagon drove on, around a curve in the road. Slowly the rug unrolled. Catman's fur was standing on end, and if he had had a tail, his tail would have been sticking straight up in the air. For a moment Catman stood still, looking at Gooney Bird. Then he ran away, very fast.

Gooney Bird sat up. She was not entirely sure what had happened. But she was not hurt. She simply wondered where her family was, and her cat, and the car.

Other cars stopped and people got out. Many people offered her a drink of water from their bottles of Evian. But Gooney Bird wasn't thirsty. After a while, a police car with a flashing light came. A TV reporter came, and a cameraman. While the policeman talked on his radio, the TV reporter, a woman with very large hair, interviewed Gooney Bird and called her "the little girl who had a flying carpet ride." In the interview, Gooney Bird described Catman and asked people to call the station if they found him. But she never got Catman back.

Eventually the police car took her to her parents, who were both crying at a gas station four miles down the road.

When Gooney Bird and her parents were finally reunited, everyone, including two policemen, a TV reporter, and the gas station owner, hugged and kissed and did the tango.

### The End

"What a lovely story!" Mrs. Pidgeon said. "And an exciting one, too! But a little sad, to lose your kitty that way."

"Catman is not a kitty," Gooney Bird said. "He is a cat. And I didn't say that I lost him. I just said that I never got him back."

"So no one found him and called the TV station?"

"Actually, they did," Gooney Bird replied.

"But where is Catman now?" asked Mrs. Pidgeon.

"He was consumed by a cow," Gooney Bird said, "but that's a different story."

"By a cow? You're joking," Mrs. Pidgeon said.

"No," said Gooney Bird. "I'm not joking. I tell only absolutely true stories."

"Tell it! Tell it!" the children called.

"I will," Gooney Bird said. "Another day."

**4.**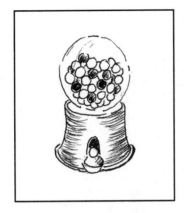

On Monday, Gooney Bird stood in front of the class when Mrs. Pidgeon told her that it was story time. The children barely noticed Gooney Bird's clothes, even though she was wearing a ruffled pinafore, dark blue knee socks, and high-top basketball sneakers. The second-graders, and Mrs. Pidgeon, too, were all much more interested in Gooney Bird's earrings.

The earrings dangled and glittered and were very large.

"They're beautiful," Keiko said in an awed voice.

"My grandma's house has doorknobs that look like that," Tricia announced. "And she has a sparkly chandelier in the dining room. My grandma is very rich."

"Do you have holes in your ears?" Malcolm asked. "My mom does. My mom went and had holes stabbed right into her ears with a needle!"

"I did, too!" Beanie called out. "I have pierced ears!"

"So do I," Mrs. Pidgeon told the class. She turned her head

from side to side so that they could all see her small gold earrings.

"No," Gooney Bird said. "My earrings screw onto my ears. They have little screws that you turn."

Barry Tuckerman thrust his arm into the air and waved it wildly. Around him, other children had their hands raised, too.

"My mom has pierced ears!" Barry said loudly.

"Ben?" Mrs. Pidgeon said next.

Ben said, "My mom has pierced ears and so does my grandma!"

"All right, class," Mrs. Pidgeon said. "Does anyone else have something to say which is *not* about pierced ears? Because it is time for Gooney Bird to begin today's story."

All of the hands disappeared except one. Chelsea kept her hand high in the air.

Mrs. Pidgeon sighed. "Chelsea?"

"My mom has a pierced *nose*," Chelsea told the class.

"Oh, no!" Keiko wailed. "I'm going to be sick!"

"Shhhh," the other children said.

When the class was quiet, Gooney Bird began her Monday story.

## The Prince, the Palace, and
## the Diamond Earrings

Once upon a time, before she moved to Watertower, when she still lived in China, Gooney Bird Greene was on her front porch, playing Monopoly against herself. Gooney Bird #1, the thimble, owned all four railroads and St. Charles Place, which she liked because it was magenta.

Gooney Bird #2, the car, was having a harder time of it. She owned Atlantic Avenue and Pennsylvania Avenue, and she liked the combination of yellow and green; she also owned both Water Works and the Electric Company, but unfortunately she was in jail.

Suddenly, just as Gooney Bird #2 tried unsuccessfully for the second time to throw doubles and get out of jail, she heard someone calling loudly, "Napoleon is missing!"

It was the prince, who lived next door.

Hands flew up into the air, and Gooney Bird looked impatiently at her classmates.

"Are these really, *really* important questions?" she asked. "Because I have just barely started the story!"

One by one most of the hands went back down.

Mrs. Pidgeon had picked up the encyclopedia. "Gooney Bird," Mrs. Pidgeon said, "I have a feeling you know this already, but Napoleon Bonaparte —" She turned to the class. "He was the emperor of France," she explained.

"Ooooh," Keiko said. "I love emperors."

Mrs. Pidgeon, still looking at the encyclopedia, went on. "Napoleon was born in 1769. That's more than two hundred years ago."

"Mrs. Pidgeon! Mrs. Pidgeon!" Barry Tuckerman was halfway out of his seat, waving his hand.

"Yes, Barry?"

"My grandmother once saw an emperor butterfly! But now it's extinct! It was purple," Barry Tuckerman said.

Gooney Bird sighed. "Do you want to hear this story or not?" she asked. "I can't wear these earrings all day. They're very heavy."

"Yes, we do," Mrs. Pidgeon said. "Please go on."

"Ready?" Gooney Bird asked the class.

Everyone was ready, so Gooney Bird continued.

"Gooney Bird," the prince called, sounding very distressed, "Napoleon has disappeared! Can you help us find him?"

Gooney Bird carefully tucked all of the Monopoly money under the edge of the board so that it wouldn't blow away. There was a slight breeze. She had had problems with money blowing away in the past. She kept her own money collection, which she carried with her at all times, safely contained in a Ziploc bag.

Then Gooney Bird set out to look for clues that might reveal the whereabouts of Napoleon.

Napoleon was not the emperor of France. He was a large black poodle.

Every hand in the second grade classroom shot up, even Felicia Ann's.

"I *knew* that would happen," Gooney Bird said. "I just knew it. Time for an intermission. Mrs. Pidgeon, do you want to deal with this?"

Mrs. Pidgeon nodded. She thought for a moment. Then she announced, "Every child who has a poodle, put your hand down."

Four hands went down.

"Now," Mrs. Pidgeon said, "every child whose grandmother has a poodle? Hands down."

Seven more hands were lowered.

"Every child who knows a poodle who does interesting tricks, or who gets into trouble, or who ran away once? Hands down."

Other hands went down, and now there were just three hands still in the air.

"Beanie? What kind of dog do you have?" Mrs. Pidgeon asked.

"Golden retriever."

"That's lovely. Ben?"

"Corgi."

"Good. And finally, Tricia?"

"I don't have a dog," Tricia said sadly. "I'm allergic to dogs. And my mother said I can never, ever have one, or even a cat, not *ever*, because I might have a terrible asthma attack, and then I would have to go to the hospital, maybe in an ambulance, and —"

"We understand, Tricia. And now let's go back to the story, because we *still* don't know what happened to Napoleon, or —"

"Or about the palace!" said Keiko. "And the earrings!"

Gooney Bird shook her head a little so that the earrings moved and sparkled in a glamorous way.

"Listen for the word *suddenly*," Gooney Bird advised. "I put one in the story already, but I like to sprinkle in several. Some other *suddenly*s will be coming soon."

Gooney Bird examined the prince's back yard. She saw a place where the ground was disturbed by the corner of the fence.

"Look," she said. "See this bit of dog hair caught in the fence? That looks like Napoleon's.

"See?" she said next, pointing to some newly dug earth. "Here is where Napoleon wiggled under the fence."

"What a good detective you are," the prince said to Gooney Bird.

Gooney Bird let herself out of the yard and through the gate. She sniffed. She listened.

Suddenly —

"There's a *suddenly*!" called Malcolm.
"Good listening," Gooney Bird said. Then she continued.

Suddenly, because of the clues that she smelled and heard, Gooney Bird moved forward. There, at the end of the alley, was an overturned garbage can. And there, with his head inside the can, was Napoleon, eating garbage. He had coffee grounds all over his face, and an orange peel was stuck on one of his ears.

"You naughty thing, Napoleon," Gooney Bird said, and she took hold of his collar. Napoleon burped.

"Oh, no!" Keiko cried. "Not *garbage*! Not *burping*!"

"Shhhh," the other children said. Many hands were waving in the air.

Mrs. Pidgeon stood up. "No stories about dogs eating garbage," she said firmly. "Not a single one."

All of the hands went down.

"Please, please, please tell about the palace and the prince and the earrings," Chelsea begged.

"I'm about to," Gooney Bird said.

Gooney Bird took Napoleon back to his house. The prince asked Gooney Bird to go to the palace for a reward.

"Did you get all dressed up in a ball gown?" Beanie asked.

"Maybe a tiara?" asked Tricia.

"I hadn't planned to describe clothes," Gooney Bird said, "but since you asked, I'll insert a little descriptive passage here."

When she went to the palace, Gooney Bird was wearing clothes from the L.L.Bean catalogue. She wore Island Hopper shorts with front flap pockets, and a pointelle knit tank top in Sun Yellow.

The prince had on rugged canvas shorts and polyester and nylon pale khaki plaid short-sleeved . . .

Malcolm disappeared under his desk. Ben picked up his arithmetic book and began to do some problems. Nicholas put his head down on his arms and closed his eyes.

Gooney Bird stared at them. "Am I boring you?" she asked.

"Yes," the class said. All but Felicia Ann, who was silent, and Keiko, who was not bored at all.

"What color were the Island Hopper shorts?" Keiko asked. "I hope blue."

"As a matter of fact, they were Deep Sea Green, with True Blue stripes down the sides. I might wear them to school on Wednesday."

"Oh good," Keiko said.

"I'll continue now," Gooney Bird said.

It doesn't matter what clothes the prince had. The main character in this story is Gooney Bird, and it is important to tell a lot about the main character because the main character is right smack in the middle of everything. All the others are just minor characters and it is boring to tell about their clothes.

"Or you could call them *secondary characters*," Mrs. Pidgeon pointed out. "Excuse me for interrupting, Gooney Bird. But I'll just write that on the board: *secondary characters*."

Gooney Bird waited patiently while Mrs. Pidgeon wrote. Then she breathed deeply and was about to continue. But she looked at the class.

She walked down the classroom aisle to Malcolm's desk and peered under it. Malcolm was asleep on the floor.

Ben was doing his arithmetic, and Nicholas was making his thumbs wrestle with each other. His left one was winning.

"This is my fault," Gooney Bird said loudly. "I have failed to hold your attention. Of course it didn't help that Mrs. Pidgeon interrupted. But I blame myself for not inserting enough suspense into the story.

"Stories need suspense," Gooney Bird said. "So I shall try to add some. Shall I continue the story now?"

"Yes," Mrs. Pidgeon said.

"Yes," said the children, all but Malcolm, who was still asleep, and Felicia Ann, who never said anything.

So Gooney Bird continued. "I'll start right off with a *suddenly*," she said. "That always wakes people up."

Suddenly, when they entered the palace, Gooney Bird needed to go to the bathroom.

Malcolm woke up. He popped up from under his desk. "I have to go to the bathroom," he said.

"Go," Mrs. Pidgeon told him, and pointed to the classroom door. Malcolm hurried from the classroom.

"Did the palace have bathrooms?" Beanie asked. "Oh, I'm sorry," she added. "I forgot to raise my hand."

"Yes," Gooney Bird said. "The palace had two bathrooms. Gentlemen and Ladies."

"And what about the diamond earrings?" Tricia asked.

"I'll finish the story now," Gooney Bird said.

When she came out of the ladies' room, Gooney Bird Greene saw a gumball machine.

"In a *palace*?" Keiko said.

"Shhhh," the other children said.

Gooney Bird continued.

Gooney Bird had not had a gumball for at least four months. She wanted one. And she had brought her money collection, since she always carried it everywhere in a very heavy Ziploc bag.

Her arms had developed big muscles from carrying her money collection.

Gooney Bird stopped the story for a moment and held up her arms to display the muscles. Then she went on.

So Gooney Bird took a penny from her money collection and put it into the gumball machine. But instead of a gumball, out came a diamond earring! It was quite a pleasant surprise, and she screwed it onto her left ear.

After that, she felt lopsided. But she could see that there was *another* diamond earring inside the gumball machine.

So she put in another penny. She got a blue gumball.

"It probably matched the True Blue stripes in her Sea Green shorts," Keiko pointed out in a loud whisper.

"Shhhh," said the class.

Gooney Bird continued.

Gooney Bird put the blue gumball into her mouth. It made a large lump in her cheek, and it tasted like spearmint.

She felt doubly lopsided now.

So she took another penny from her money collection and put it into the gumball machine. This time she got a yellow gumball. She put the yellow gumball into her mouth, and now she had a large lump on either side of her face, so her face wasn't lopsided, but her *head* still felt lopsided because she had only one diamond earring.

So she put another penny in, and she got a red gumball. She put it into her pocket to save for later. Now her hips felt lopsided. She took another penny from her money collection.

This time she got an orange gumball and put it into her other pocket, and now her hips weren't lopsided anymore, but she still had only one diamond earring.

Gooney Bird stopped the story and looked at the class. "I am going to jump ahead now," she said. "Mrs. Pidgeon, is there a word for when an author jumps ahead in a story and skips over some things?"

Mrs. Pidgeon thought about it. "When an author jumps

*backward* in a story, it is called a 'flashback.' So maybe jumping ahead would be called a 'flash-forward'?"

"Well," Gooney Bird announced, "I am flashing forward."

After twenty minutes, all of the pennies in Gooney Bird's money collection were gone. And the gumball machine was empty. Now Gooney Bird had sixty-seven gumballs: two in her mouth, two in her pockets, and sixty-three in her Ziploc bag.

Also, she had a pair of very large, glittery, dangly diamond earrings, which she wears to this day.

When they saw her in the diamond earrings, everyone in the palace, including the prince, two motorcycle guys, and a lady in a wheelchair, cheered. Then they hugged and kissed and did a short but quite beautiful ballet.

The End

"What a lovely story!" Mrs. Pidgeon said. "And the flash-forward was very effective, Gooney Bird. I'm so glad you finally got the second earring."

Gooney Bird turned her head from side to side so her

classmates could admire the earrings. All of the children clapped.

"Did the prince ask you to marry him?" Keiko asked.

"What are you talking about?" Gooney Bird said. "The Prinns are already married. Mr. Howard Prinn is married to Mrs. Amanda Prinn. One Prinn plus one Prinn equals *Prinns*. The Prinns lived next door to me with their dog, Napoleon."

"Oh," the children said. *"Prinns."*

Barry Tuckerman had jumped up and was waving his arm frantically in the air.

"That wasn't a true story!" Barry called out.

"I tell only absolutely true stories," Gooney Bird said impatiently. "How many times must I tell you that?"

"No, it wasn't, because I've seen lots of pictures of palaces, and they have throne rooms, and red carpets, and people get dressed up in ball gowns, and —"

"Barry, Barry, Barry," Gooney Bird said with a sigh. "What am I going to do with you?"

"What do you mean?" Barry asked.

"You're talking about a small-p palace. But I was talking about a capital-letter ice cream shop called The Palace, where they have —"

"Bathrooms!" Beanie suggested.

"And a gumball machine!" Chelsea said. "With diamond earrings!"

"Exactly right," Gooney Bird said, and she took her seat. Then carefully she unscrewed her dangling earrings. "Ouch," she said. "These really hurt."

Malcolm returned to the classroom. "Did you get out of jail, Gooney Bird?" he asked.

Gooney Bird looked unhappy for a moment. "No," she said. "Napoleon ate my Monopoly game."

**5.**

On Tuesday, all of the children, including Felicia Ann, arrived at school early — even Malcolm, who had never been early before.

Tricia had a flower in her hair.

Ben was wearing a vest.

Keiko had a tiny bit of pink lipstick on her lips.

And Barry Tuckerman was wearing a polka dot bow tie.

"Good morning, class," Mrs. Pidgeon said. "Don't you all look nice today!"

"You do, too, Mrs. Pidgeon!" the children said, and Mrs. Pidgeon blushed.

"Well," she said, "I thought I'd wear my new shoes today." Usually Mrs. Pidgeon wore soft, comfortable shoes. But today she was wearing very shiny high-heeled shoes with gold buckles.

The principal, Mr. Leroy, made announcements on the

intercom. He announced a bake sale and a birthday and a meeting of the crossing guards.

A fifth grade boy read a poem about Christopher Columbus over the intercom. Everyone in the school said the Pledge of Allegiance together. Then it was time for school to begin.

But Gooney Bird wasn't there.

"Well," Mrs. Pidgeon said, "let's take out our social studies books, class. Let's turn to the chapter called 'Cities.'"

"But Gooney Bird isn't here!" Nicholas called.

"No," Mrs. Pidgeon said, "she isn't. She seems to be absent today. Maybe she has the chicken pox."

The class was silent. The room seemed sad. The lights seemed dim. Even the gerbils, who usually scurried noisily around in their cage, were very subdued. George Washington, in his portrait on the wall, looked as if he might cry any minute.

Slowly the children took their social studies books from their desks and turned to the chapter called "Cities."

Keiko began to cry very quietly. "I don't want to do social studies," she whimpered. "I feel too sad."

Malcolm crawled under his desk and curled up in a ball.

Suddenly the door to the room burst open.

"It's Gooney Bird!" everybody called. The lights seemed to brighten. The gerbils began to run in a circle, and George Washington seemed to smile.

Gooney Bird was out of breath. "I'm sorry I'm late," she said. "I am never, ever late for anything. I always set three alarm clocks, and I lay out my clothes the night before, and I even put toothpaste on my toothbrush before I go to bed so that I can brush my teeth quickly in the morning! But today —

"Wait," she said. "I have to catch my breath." She stood in front of the class and took a few deep breaths. "There," she said. "I'm fine now."

She smoothed her red hair, which was flying about, and tucked it behind her ears. Today Gooney Bird was wearing gray sweatpants, a sleeveless white blouse with lace on the collar, and amazing black gloves that came up above her elbows.

"This morning," she explained, "I quite unexpectedly had to direct an orchestra."

"An orchestra?" asked Mrs. Pidgeon.

"Yes. A symphony orchestra."

Mrs. Pidgeon smiled. "I hear all sorts of interesting excuses for tardiness, but I have never heard that one before."

"I believe I'm unique," Gooney Bird said.

"Yes, you are, indeed. Did you wear your gloves when you were directing the orchestra?"

"Yes," said Gooney Bird, "as a matter of fact, I did. I found them very helpful."

All of the second-graders had their hands in the air and

56

were pretending to lead orchestras. Even Malcolm was back in his seat, using two pencils as orchestra batons.

Gooney Bird headed toward her desk. She looked around at the other children's open books. "I see we're in the middle of social studies," she said.

Mrs. Pidgeon slipped one foot out of a high-heeled shoe and rubbed it with her hand. Then she put her shoe back on. "Actually," she said, "I think the class would appreciate it if we held story time a little early today."

"YAY!" called all the children, and they closed up their social studies books.

"A Gooney Bird story?" Gooney Bird asked.

"Yes," said Mrs. Pidgeon.

"YES!" called all the children.

Gooney Bird smoothed her long gloves. She went back up to the front of the room. "Which one would you like today?" she asked. "'How Catman Was Consumed by a Cow'?"

"I'd certainly like to hear about Catman and the cow sometime," Mrs. Pidgeon said. "Maybe tomorrow? But this morning I'd like to hear one called 'Why Gooney Bird Was Late for School Because She Had to Direct a Symphony Orchestra.'"

"Oh," Gooney Bird said. "All right. I could tell that."

"And it will be absolutely true?" asked Mrs. Pidgeon.

"Of course," Gooney Bird said. "Have you forgotten? All of my stories are absolutely true."

Then she curtsied, and began.

## Why Gooney Bird Was Late for School Because She Was Directing a Symphony Orchestra

Once upon a time, in fact it was just this morning, Gooney Bird Greene got up and got dressed in the clothes that she had carefully laid out the night before.

She ate her breakfast, brushed her teeth with her pre-pasted toothbrush, gathered up her homework, put on her elbow-length gloves, and started off to the Watertower Elementary School.

Gooney Bird interrupted herself. She explained to the teacher and the class, "Sometimes stories start in the most ordinary way. Then they become exciting when something unexpected happens. Don't you find that to be true?"

The children nodded, thinking about their favorite stories.

"Like *Where the Wild Things Are*," Ben suggested.

"Or *Little Red Riding Hood*," Beanie said. "When the wolf appears, and you don't expect it!"

"Oh, I'm so scared of the wolf!" Keiko whispered loudly. "Every time the wolf appears, I —"

"Shhhh," the children said.

Gooney Bird continued.

Gooney Bird walked down Park Street, and turned the corner onto Walnut Street, and when she was halfway down Walnut Street, halfway to school, suddenly . . .

She paused. "I've explained before," she said, "about the word *suddenly*. It makes things exciting. Sometimes, class, if you're creating a story and you get stuck, just say the word *suddenly* and you won't have any trouble continuing at all."

"What a good idea!" Mrs. Pidgeon said. "We should start a list called 'Writing Tips.' What happened suddenly on Walnut Street, Gooney Bird?"

Gooney Bird continued.

Suddenly she saw an enormous red and white bus coming, very slowly. Each window had a head in it. The bus was quite full of people.

Gooney Bird was amazed. Even though she had lived in Watertower only a short time, about a week, she knew that the town of Watertower did not have enormous red and white buses.

Watertower had two medium-sized yellow school buses, Gooney Bird knew. And she knew, also, that one of the Watertower churches had a small white bus, really a long van, that had a rainbow painted on it, and said *JESUS IS LORD* on each side.

But an enormous red and white bus was completely new to Watertower.

As Gooney Bird watched, it moved very, very slowly down Walnut Street. She could see that the driver, though he was steering carefully, was also trying to look at a map in his hands.

The bus driver saw Gooney Bird, and he beeped his horn a very small beep. He pulled the bus to a stop with a breathy sound of brakes. Then he pushed the handle that opened the folding door.

"Excuse me?" the bus driver said. "You look as if you're on your way to school."

"Yes, I am," Gooney Bird replied, "and I certainly don't want to be late. I am never, ever late."

The bus driver looked as if he might begin to cry. "I feel exactly the same way," he said. "I am never, ever late. But this morning I have a terrible problem." He held up his unfolded map.

"Do you need help folding your map?" Gooney

Bird asked. "It *is* hard to fold a map. But I find that if you follow the creases very carefully —"

"No," the bus driver said. "My problem is that I'm lost."

"Oh, dear," Gooney Bird said.

"And," the driver continued, "we are going to be late for a concert."

"A concert?"

"Yes. I have an entire symphony orchestra on this bus."

Gooney Bird paused. "Questions about orchestras?" She asked. "Class?"

Barry Tuckerman was waving his hand wildly. "We know all the parts of an orchestra! We listened to *A Young Person's Guide to the Orchestra*!"

"Winds!" Ben called.

"Strings!" Tricia called. She pretended to play an imaginary violin.

"Brass!" Chelsea called. She tried to make a trombone noise, not very successfully.

"Percussion!" said Malcolm loudly, and he began to tap his two pencils in rhythm on his desktop.

"And also," Barry called out, his hand still waving, "we listened to *Peter and the Wolf*!"

"Oh," Keiko said in a small voice, "I hate when the wolf comes. Every time the wolf appears, I —"

"Shhhh," the children said.

Gooney Bird continued.

So Gooney Bird climbed up the steps and got on the bus.

Every seat was filled. There were men and women in the bus, all of them dressed in black. All the men were wearing black turtleneck shirts. The women were all wearing long black skirts.

They definitely looked like an orchestra. But they looked very distressed.

"Where are you supposed to go?" Gooney Bird asked the bus driver.

"To the Town Hall Auditorium," he said. "We are supposed to play a concert there this morning." He looked at his watch. "It begins in twenty minutes," he said in a worried voice.

"I will get you there," Gooney Bird said.

The bus driver called to the orchestra players.

"This wonderful girl is going to direct us!" he said.

"Yay!" the orchestra players all called.

Luckily, even though she had lived in Watertower for only a week, Gooney Bird knew exactly where the Town Hall Auditorium was, because her father had pointed it out when they drove around the town.

"There is the hospital," her father had said. "Go there if you happen to fall from a ladder and break your arm.

"There is the police station," he had said. "Go there if you happen to see a bank robber on the loose.

"And there is the Town Hall Auditorium," her father had said. "Go there if you want to see a ballet or a concert."

"Start the bus," Gooney Bird told the driver, "and turn right at the very next corner." It was a good thing that she was wearing her long black gloves. When she pointed, everyone could see her long black pointing finger.

There was no place for Gooney Bird to sit down.

And we all know that it is dangerous to stand while a bus is going. But she had no choice. She stood beside the driver and held on to the side of his seat. He promised to drive very, very carefully.

"Next, turn left," Gooney Bird said, and pointed.

"And there we are!" she told him. "See that large brick building? That is the Town Hall Auditorium!"

"Yay!" the orchestra players called again. The women began to comb their hair.

"Thank you for directing us!" they all said to Gooney Bird as they got out of the bus. The driver had opened the luggage compartment and was lifting out cellos.

"You will be late to school," one man said as he picked up a large black case. "Trombone," he explained.

"Yes, I will," Gooney Bird said. "I will be tardy."

"Is there some way that we can thank you for leading our orchestra?" he asked.

Gooney Bird thought for a moment. Finally she thought of a way, and she whispered it to the trombone player.

He nodded. "Yes," he said. "We will do that."

One by one the musicians thanked Gooney Bird. She said goodbye and hurried down the street to Watertower Elementary School.

She arrived at school just as the class was about to read "Cities" in their social studies books.

## The End

"Questions, anyone?" Gooney Bird asked.

"Was there a drum player?" Malcolm asked.

"Yes," Gooney Bird said. "Every single part of a symphony orchestra was there. Even a harp."

"Oh," Malcolm said, sighing. "I wish I could have seen the drum player. I love drums."

"You will," Gooney Bird said.

"Was there a flute player?" Chelsea asked.

"Two," Gooney Bird said.

"I wish I could hear the flute players," Chelsea said.

"You will," Gooney Bird said.

"I have a question, Gooney Bird," Mrs. Pidgeon said. "What was it that you whispered to the trombone player?"

"Secret," Gooney Bird said. "But you'll find out at twelve o'clock sharp."

"That's lunchtime," Mrs. Pidgeon pointed out.

"Precisely," Gooney Bird said. "Now, shall we turn to our social studies?"

All morning the children, and Mrs. Pidgeon, too, glanced again and again at the big clock on the wall. They did social studies and arithmetic and had a snack in the middle of the morning. Then they did reading and art. Finally, just as the clock hands moved to twelve o'clock and the second-graders were about to reach for their lunch boxes, Gooney Bird announced, "Here they are!"

She pointed to the large windows on the side of the classroom. The children all stood up and watched though the windows as a red and white bus pulled up and parked.

When the door of the bus opened, the orchestra players came out one by one, holding their instruments. They arranged themselves in a semicircle on the lawn, facing the Watertower Elementary School.

The conductor, holding a baton, stepped to the center and lifted his arms.

"Too bad he doesn't have long black gloves," Gooney Bird murmured.

Mrs. Pidgeon opened the windows so that they could hear better. The orchestra began to play a slow, stately melody.

When it was finished, the conductor bowed. Then he turned to the windows and explained, "That was a sarabande. It's a kind of dance. We'll play it one more time, in honor of Gooney Bird Greene."

So the orchestra played the short sarabande again, and the children danced around the classroom in a very serious and graceful way.

**6.**

"Today," Gooney Bird said on Wednesday, "I am going to tell you about Catman and the cow. Maybe you've noticed that I'm wearing my cat and cow outfit today."

The students nodded their heads. They *had* noticed. Gooney Bird was wearing an orange fur jacket. Over her shoulder was slung a purse made from brown and white cowhide.

"Sometimes storytellers have special outfits that they wear. I think that's fine as long as it doesn't interfere with the story," Gooney Bird continued. "You can buy fake cat whiskers and ears, for example. But I would never wear such a distracting costume."

"Would you wear a tail?" Beanie asked. "I know somebody who had a cat tail and ears at Halloween."

"Put on your thinking caps, class," Gooney Bird said. "Think back to when I talked about Catman last week."

"*No tail!*" the entire class said, all except Felicia Ann,

although she looked up from the floor.

"That's right. Catman has no tail. I would tell about the lawn mower accident and it would be an absolutely true story, but I never use violence in my stories."

"Oh, good," Keiko said. "Violence makes me cry."

Gooney Bird smoothed her fur jacket and did her breathing exercises. Deep breath. Let it out. Deep breath. Let it out. "I know a lot of you have been worried about Catman," she began.

"I certainly have," Mrs. Pidgeon said. "I've been thinking about Catman ever since he flew out of that flying carpet."

"By the way, Mrs. Pidgeon," Gooney Bird said, "I do want to mention how lovely you look today."

Mrs. Pidgeon blushed a little. She was still wearing her high-heeled shoes with the buckles, and today she was also wearing a rhinestone butterfly perched in her hair.

"In fact, the whole class looks quite lovely," Gooney Bird pointed out. She looked around. "Malcolm, would you stand up?"

Malcolm rose from his seat and held his shoulders back. He was still wearing his polka dot bow tie, and today he had added a plaid belt.

"Keiko?" Gooney Bird said.

Keiko giggled and stood. She had a bright green bow in her hair and a long shiny silk scarf wrapped around her neck.

"Me?" called Chelsea. "Can I stand up?" She did, and the

class could see that she was wearing a fringed cowboy vest over her best dress.

"Me! Me!" Everyone, all but Felicia Ann, was calling out now, but Gooney Bird said, "Later. After the story. I'm ready to begin now."

She took one more deep breath, let it out, and began.

## Beloved Catman Is Consumed by a Cow

Once upon a time, not long ago, after they had left China, Gooney Bird and Catman found themselves flying through the air on a carpet. The carpet landed in a meadow, near a large brown and white cow who was contentedly eating wildflowers. The flowers were purple loosestrife.

The carpet unrolled, and Gooney Bird stood up and looked around. She could see, in the distance, her father's car quickly disappearing down the road.

Beside her, Catman also stood up. He had become very furry and fat, the way cats do when they are frightened.

"My cat becomes very enlarged when my brother brings his dog to visit," Mrs. Pidgeon said. Then she put her hand to her mouth. "Oh! I'm sorry, Gooney Bird. I interrupted."

"That's all right," Gooney Bird replied. "Maybe this is a good time for everyone to tell cat-getting-big-suddenly stories."

Many children did. Barry Tuckerman's grandmother's cat became huge and his tail stood straight out in the air when a groundhog appeared in the yard.

Chelsea's cat became enormously fluffy and hissed and spat when the veterinarian gave her a shot.

Tricia told how her cat got very, very fat and then one day had seven kittens inside the laundry basket.

"Good. So you all understand about cats. Now I'll continue," Gooney Bird announced.

The cow, who had some purple blossoms dangling from her mouth, looked very surprised when a person and a cat and a carpet all landed in her meadow. She thought about what to do and decided that moving to a different corner of the meadow would be the best choice. Carefully, moving slowly in a cowlike fashion, she strolled away toward a corner where yellow cosmos and oxeye daisies were in bloom.

Gooney Bird's attention was on the car, which had now disappeared around a bend in the road. She was a little worried about the disappearance of the car.

But Catman didn't care about the car. Catman had never liked the car at all. In fact, Catman had *hated* the car, and he was glad that it had disappeared.

But he was very interested in the cow. Catman had never seen a cow before. Now he watched with fascination as the cow moved slowly toward the other corner of the meadow.

He liked the way the cow walked, heavily and with determination.

He liked the way the cow smelled, of thick, sun-warmed cowhide and meadow flowers.

And, as he scampered along behind the cow and the cow noticed and mooed, Catman liked the way the cow *sounded*. It was comforting, the low, throaty sound of a moo, and in the background was the buzzing of flies.

Catman began to purr. In the distance, he could

hear Gooney Bird calling "Catman! Catman!" But he didn't care. He found himself falling in love with the cow.

"I like romance," Beanie said.
"Me too," Keiko said with a tiny sigh.
Gooney Bird waited a moment, but no one else said anything. She continued the story.

In the evening, the farmer, Mr. Henry Schinhofen, came to the meadow and called the cow. It was time to take her into the barn to be milked.

The cow liked the farmer, who was soft-spoken and kind; and she liked the barn, which was airy and dark and smelled of hay; and she liked being milked, which felt a little like sneezing: something that needs to be done now and then. So she cheerfully followed the farmer when he called her.

Catman cheerfully followed the cow.

Mrs. Clara Schinhofen, the farmer's wife, was feeding the chickens when her husband walked past, leading the cow. "My word," she said.

"Look! There's a cat with no tail, following the cow!"

"So there is," said her husband. "Perhaps he is hungry. We should feed him."

They tried to take Catman into the house to be fed, but he refused to leave the cow. So they brought him a bowl of tuna fish and gave it to him in the barn. When Mr. Schinhofen milked the cow, he squirted some into a dish for Catman.

That night, Catman, who was by now completely and hopelessly in love, curled up beside the cow and slept. He has slept there ever since. During the day, he goes to the meadow with the cow, and while the cow eats wildflowers, Catman chases field mice and butterflies, listens to the buzzing of flies, and smells the warm and pleasant odor of cowhide.

Gooney Bird paused. "Questions?" she said.

Keiko raised her hand. "I was waiting for the bad part," she said. "I was going to cover my ears."

"What bad part?" asked Gooney Bird.

"You know," Keiko whispered. "Where the cow ate Catman."

Gooney Bird looked surprised. "The cow didn't eat Catman! The cow hardly notices that Catman is there! The cow eats wildflowers."

"But you said —" Keiko began.

"Yes! You said —" Malcolm called.

Mrs. Pidgeon stood up. "Remember the title of the story, children," she said.

They all tried. "'How a Cow Ate Catman,'" Barry Tuckerman called out.

"'How Catman Got Eaten Up by a Cow,'" Tricia said.

Mrs. Pidgeon shook her head. She picked up her notebook. "I wrote it down," she told them. "'Beloved Catman Is Consumed by a Cow.'"

"Let me finish," Gooney Bird suggested. She went on with the end of the story.


That night the farmer and his wife turned on the TV and saw the interview with the little girl who rode a flying carpet.

"If anybody finds my cat," the little girl (it was Gooney Bird) said, "please call the TV station."

So Mr. Henry Schinhofen, the farmer, called.

"I have that cat here in my barn," he said.

"Orange and white cat, no tail.

"But I gotta tell you," he said, "I don't think you'll be able to take it away. It won't leave my cow."

"Won't leave your cow?" the TV lady said. She sounded puzzled.

"Nope," said the farmer. "Wouldn't even leave for tuna fish. We had to take the tuna fish and put it right beside the cow."

"Why?"

"Happens sometimes," the farmer explained. "I'd guess you'd call it something like love. That cat is downright consumed by the cow."

"And is the cow consumed by the cat?" the TV lady asked.

"Nope. The cow doesn't care one way or another. But she doesn't step on the cat. She's a careful cow."

The TV people called Gooney Bird and her parents. They told them where Catman was, and that Catman was consumed by a cow.

So the Greene family drove their car back to the meadow and visited Catman. Catman was nice to

them, but they could tell that he was not consumed by the Greene family. He was consumed
only by the cow.

So they kissed him goodbye. Then they hugged
and kissed the farmer and his wife, and they all
sang "Farmer in the Dell" and danced in a circle,
on their tiptoes. They all lived happily ever after.

## The End

"I love happy endings," Keiko said with a sigh.

"Me too," Mrs. Pidgeon said. "Thank you, Gooney Bird.
Let's get out our arithmetic books now, class."

Everyone in the class groaned.

"I know," Mrs. Pidgeon said, laughing. "It's much more
fun to listen to Gooney Bird's stories. But we can look forward to tomorrow. She'll have another one tomorrow."

Gooney Bird had gone back to her desk and taken out her
arithmetic book. She looked up in surprise. "No, actually I
won't," she said. "That was my last story."

The second-graders, almost every one of them, called,
"No!" in very loud, sad voices. It sounded like a huge chorus
singing a song called "Noooooo!"

Mrs. Pidgeon looked horrified. "But, Gooney Bird!" she
said. "We still have a lot of unanswered questions!"

"Like what?" asked Gooney Bird.

"Well, let me think." Mrs. Pidgeon frowned.

"The false teeth!" Nicholas called.

"Yes," Mrs. Pidgeon said. "Why did your father have to pack forty-three sets of false teeth? That's a story you haven't told yet."

Gooney Bird looked surprised. "That's not a story," she said. "That simply requires a dictionary. You have one right there on your desk, Mrs. Pidgeon."

Mrs. Pidgeon reached for her dictionary.

"Look up this word," Gooney Bird said. She pronounced the word very carefully. *"Prosthodontist."*

"My goodness!" Mrs. Pidgeon read the definition. "It's a special kind of dentist. He makes false teeth!"

"Exactly," Gooney Bird said. "That's what my father is. No story there."

"But we want more stories, Gooney Bird!" Barry Tuckerman said in a loud voice. As usual, he was standing up with one knee on his desk chair.

Gooney Bird sighed impatiently. "I need to do my arithmetic," she said. "I'm not very good at subtraction yet. But all right. Sit down, Barry. Close the dictionary, Mrs. Pidgeon. I will tell you how to get stories."

**7.**

Gooney Bird looked around the classroom. She slid the strap of her cowhide purse from her shoulder and set the purse on the floor below the terrarium table. With her face scrunched into a quiet, thinking expression, she unbuttoned her orange fur jacket and hung it on the back of the chair by her desk. Then she returned to the front of the room and faced the class.

She was wearing a blue plaid skirt, a white blouse, black tights, and brown lace-up shoes. There were bright blue hair ribbons in her neatly brushed red hair. She looked ordinary. She looked dignified. She looked wise.

"Out there, invisible, are a lot of stories not yet told," Gooney Bird told the class.

"Absolutely true ones?" Beanie asked in a small voice.

"Yes. Absolutely true ones."

"What are they?" asked Beanie.

"Do you remember that my first story was called 'How

Gooney Bird Got Her Name'?" Gooney Bird asked.

"Yes," Beanie replied.

"Well, another is called 'How Beanie Got Her Name.'"

"Before I was born," Beanie said, laughing, "there was a thing called an ultrasound that showed me curled up inside my mom? And I looked just like a bean! My mom said lima bean, and my daddy said no, jelly bean, and so —"

"That's a fine story beginning," Gooney Bird said. "An absolutely true one. You should tell that one on Friday, Beanie."

"What other invisible stories are out there?" Mrs. Pidgeon asked.

"Do you remember that my second story was about how I came from China on a flying carpet?"

"Oh my, yes," Mrs. Pidgeon said. "I had to look up *China* in the atlas."

"Out there, invisible, and waiting," Gooney Bird said, "is a story called — let me think." She closed her eyes.

"Is that the title? 'Let Me Think'?" Malcolm asked.

"No." Gooney Bird opened her eyes. "The story is called 'How Keiko's Family Came to Watertower.'"

Keiko smiled. "Well, they started out on a ship," she said. "First my grandmother and grandfather got on a big ship in Yokohama and went to Honolulu. They were a little scared because they had never been to America before. Mrs. Pidgeon, you should get the atlas out."

Mrs. Pidgeon smiled. "I will, when you tell your story, Keiko. Maybe next Wednesday?"

"Okay," Keiko said. "And I'll bring some pictures. And how about if I wear a kimono? That wouldn't be distracting, like whiskers, would it?"

"It would be lovely," Gooney Bird said.

"And I could maybe carry a fan, and a parasol?"

Gooney Bird said gently, "That would be a little like whiskers, Keiko."

"Overdoing it?" Keiko asked.

"Overdoing it," Gooney Bird said.

"What about *me*?" asked Barry. "Do I have a story?"

"Of course you do," Gooney Bird told him. "You have stories called 'How Barry Got His Name' and 'How Barry's Family Came to Watertower' and lots of others."

Barry grinned. "Which one should I tell?" he asked.

"Do you remember that my third story was about my diamond earrings?"

Barry nodded.

"My suggestion is that when it's your turn, Barry, you should tell an absolutely true story called 'When Barry Spent Every Penny He Had on Something He Wanted Really Badly.'"

The class waited and watched Barry Tuckerman as he squinched his face up, thinking. Then he grinned.

"Okay," he said. "I'll tell it! But it's really, really gross."

"Oh, no!" said Keiko. "I hate gross."

"You can cover your ears for Barry's story," Gooney Bird told her. "Wear earmuffs that day. Green ones would go nicely with your red sweater, I think."

"Who else? What else?" the class called.

"My fourth story was called 'How Gooney Bird Directed an Orchestra.'"

Mrs. Pidgeon suggested, "Maybe we could skip that one, Gooney Bird. I know no one in the class has ever led an orchestra."

"Class?" Gooney Bird asked. "Has anyone here ever been late to school because something quite unusual happened?"

Almost every hand went up.

"Malcolm," Gooney Bird said, "maybe that story could be your assignment. It could be called 'Why Malcolm Was Late to School.'"

"It could be about the time I was asleep under my bed and my mother couldn't find me in the morning," Malcolm said, "or the time that I dropped my toothbrush in the toilet and when I tried to get it back I —"

"Oh, no!" Keiko cried, and covered her ears.

"Don't tell it now and give it away, Malcolm," Gooney Bird said. "You work on your story, and make it very suspenseful by adding a *suddenly* in the middle."

Gooney Bird looked around the classroom. All the second-graders had taken out paper and pencils. They were all writing down ideas for their stories.

"And remember my last story, about Catman?" she reminded them. "Has anyone here ever lost a beloved pet?"

Almost every hand went up again. Even Mrs. Pidgeon's.

"Could that be my story, Gooney Bird?" Mrs. Pidgeon said. "I had a parakeet named Brucie, and somehow the door to his cage was left open, and —"

"Next Tuesday," Gooney Bird said. "'How I Lost Brucie.'"

"'And Found Him Again,'" Mrs. Pidgeon said with a happy smile. "My story has a surprise ending."

"Mine will be 'How I Lost Gretchen Guinea Pig,'" Tricia said. "Mine has a sad ending."

"You know what?" Mrs. Pidgeon said, standing up. "It's lunchtime already. Let's skip arithmetic today, class."

The students put the arithmetic books back in their desks. They reached for lunch boxes instead.

Gooney Bird took out a grapefruit, a cucumber, and some dill pickles. "I'm having a completely vegetarian day today," she explained. "But look at this! Dessert! For the whole class!"

She held up a bulky paper bag.

"What is it?" the children asked.

Gooney Bird grinned. "Sixty-three gumballs," she said. "And after I give them out, I am going to teach you all a wonderful whirling dance called the tarantella."

Suddenly Felicia Ann looked up from the floor. "Shouldn't

we all hug and kiss first?" she said in a surprisingly loud voice.

"Thank you for suggesting that, Felicia Ann," Gooney Bird replied. "Of course we should." And so they did.

The End